USBORNE HOTSHOTS

FLAGS

USBORNE HOTSHOTS

FLAGS

William Crampton

Edited by Lisa Miles
Designed by Nigel Reece and Fiona Johnson

Illustrated by Radhi Parekh
Flag images generated by the Flag Institute

Series editor: Judy Tatchell
Series designer: Ruth Russell

Additional illustration by Guy Smith

CONTENTS

About flags

There are over 180 nations in the world and all of them have their own national flag. Many other groups and organizations have flags to represent them too.

National flags

When you see a national flag, whether on a building, at a sports match or on television, look through this book until you find it.

For each flag you spot, mark the box next to its picture in the book. The date tells you when it was first used. There is an example on the right. If you are not sure where a country is in the world, you could look it up in an atlas.

New Zealand
☐ June 12, 1902

New nations

The flags of the world change frequently. New flags are invented as new countries are born, or their situation changes. For instance, the government of South Africa changed dramatically in 1994 when all the adults in the country were allowed to vote in free elections for the first time. To celebrate South Africa's new identity, a new flag was designed.

New flag of South Africa

South African flag until 1994

Back and front

Flags have a front, called the obverse, and a back called the reverse. The obverse is the side you see when the pole, or flagstaff, is on the left. In this book, flags shown without flagstaffs are all obverse. The reverse is usually a mirror-image.

The flag of Guyana

Reverse

Obverse

The parts of a flag

Flags are usually made of cloth, with patterns made by sewing or printing. At one side of the cloth is a piece of material, called a sleeve. This is used to attach the flag to the flagstaff. There are many ways of doing this, but here is the simplest.

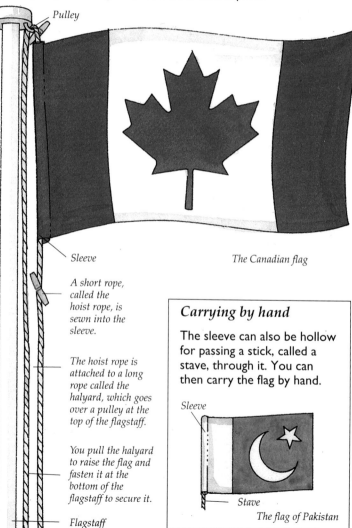

Pulley

Sleeve

The Canadian flag

A short rope, called the *hoist rope*, is sewn into the sleeve.

The hoist rope is attached to a long rope called the *halyard*, which goes over a pulley at the top of the flagstaff.

You pull the halyard to raise the flag and fasten it at the bottom of the flagstaff to secure it.

Flagstaff

Carrying by hand

The sleeve can also be hollow for passing a stick, called a stave, through it. You can then carry the flag by hand.

Sleeve

Stave

The flag of Pakistan

5

Africa

Algeria
☐ November 1, 1954

Angola
☐ November 11, 1975

Benin
☐ August 1, 1990

Botswana
☐ September 30, 1966

Burkina Faso
☐ August 4, 1984

Burundi
☐ June 28, 1967

Cameroon
☐ May 20, 1975

Cape Verde
☐ September 25, 1992

Central African Rep.*
☐ December 1, 1958

Chad
☐ November 6, 1959

Comoros
☐ October 1, 1978

Congo
☐ June 10, 1991

Côte d'Ivoire
☐ December 3, 1959

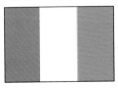

Djibouti
☐ June 27, 1977

Egypt
☐ October 4, 1984

*Rep. stands for Republic.

6

Equatorial Guinea
☐ October 12, 1968

Eritrea
☐ May 24, 1993

Ethiopia
☐ August 6, 1897

Gabon
☐ August 9, 1960

Gambia
☐ February 18, 1965

Ghana
☐ March 6, 1967

Guinea
☐ November 10, 1958

Guinea-Bissau
☐ September 24, 1973

Kenya
☐ December 12, 1963

Lesotho
☐ January 19, 1987

Liberia
☐ August 27, 1847

Libya
☐ March 1977

Madagascar
☐ October 14, 1958

Malawi
☐ July 6, 1964

Mali
☐ March 1, 1961

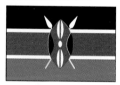

Mauritania
☐ April 1, 1959

Mauritius
☐ January 9, 1968

Morocco
☐ November 10, 1917

Mozambique
☐ May 1, 1983

Namibia
☐ March 21, 1990

Niger
☐ November 23, 1959

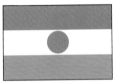

Nigeria
☐ October 1, 1960

Rwanda
☐ September 1961

São Tomé & Príncipe
☐ July 12, 1975

Senegal
☐ August 22, 1960

Seychelles
☐ June 18, 1996

Sierra Leone
☐ April 27, 1961

Somalia
☐ October 12, 1954

South Africa
☐ April 27, 1994

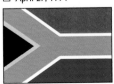

Sudan
☐ May 20, 1970

Tunisia ☐ 1835

This is one of the oldest flags in continuous use in Africa. The crescent and star is the badge of Islam and was originally used by Turkey, to which Tunisia belonged.

Swaziland
☐ October 30, 1967

Tanzania
☐ June 1964

Togo
☐ April 27, 1960

Uganda
☐ October 9, 1962

Zaire
☐ November 20, 1971

Zambia
☐ October 24, 1964

Zimbabwe

The bird in the triangle is a picture of a carving found in the ruins of Great Zimbabwe – a city that existed 500 years ago.

April 18, 1980

Asia

Afghanistan
☐ December 2, 1992

Bahrain
☐ 1932

Bangladesh
☐ April 1972

Bhutan
☐ 1965

Brunei
☐ September 29, 1959

Cambodia
☐ September 23, 1993

India

This flag is based on that of the Indian National Congress
Party, which campaigned for independence from Britain. This
was achieved in 1947. The wheel symbol comes from an
ancient carving in northern India. It is
a symbol of the great Indian
civilizations of the past.

☐ July 22, 1947

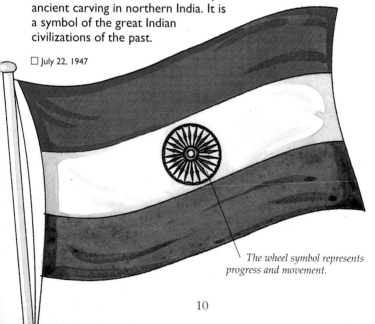

*The wheel symbol represents
progress and movement.*

China
☐ October 1, 1949

Indonesia
☐ January 27, 1949

Iran
☐ July 29, 1980

Iraq
☐ January 14, 1991

Israel
☐ October 28, 1948

Japan
☐ January 27, 1870

Jordan
☐ April 16, 1928

Kazakhstan
☐ June 4, 1992

Korea, North
☐ September 9, 1948

Korea, South
☐ September 8, 1948

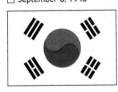

Kuwait
☐ September 7, 1961

Kyrgyzstan
☐ March 3, 1992

Laos
☐ December 2, 1975

Lebanon
☐ December 1, 1941

Malaysia
☐ September 16, 1963

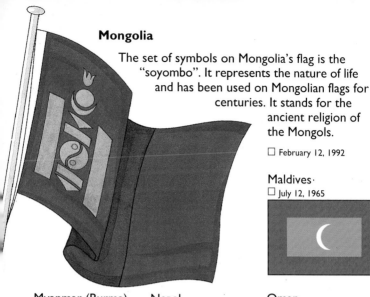

Mongolia

The set of symbols on Mongolia's flag is the "soyombo". It represents the nature of life and has been used on Mongolian flags for centuries. It stands for the ancient religion of the Mongols.

☐ February 12, 1992

Maldives·
☐ July 12, 1965

Myanmar (Burma)
☐ January 4, 1974

Nepal
☐ December 16, 1962

Oman
☐ April 25, 1995

Pakistan
☐ August 11, 1947

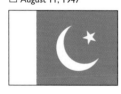

Philippines
☐ May 19, 1898

Qatar
☐ 1949

Saudi Arabia
☐ 1973

Sri Lanka
☐ December 17, 1978

Syria
☐ March 29, 1980

12

Singapore

On this flag, the crescent stands for a new, young country. The five stars represent the ideals it hopes to achieve. On many other flags, the crescent stands for Islam, but not in this case.

☐ December 3, 1959

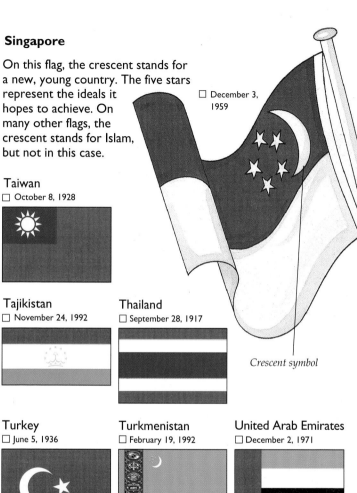

Crescent symbol

Taiwan
☐ October 8, 1928

Tajikistan
☐ November 24, 1992

Thailand
☐ September 28, 1917

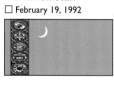

Turkey
☐ June 5, 1936

Turkmenistan
☐ February 19, 1992

United Arab Emirates
☐ December 2, 1971

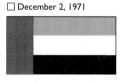

Uzbekistan
☐ March 18, 1991

Vietnam
☐ November 30, 1955

Yemen
☐ May 22, 1990

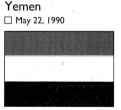

13

Australasia

Australia
☐ May 22, 1909

Fiji
☐ October 10, 1970

Kiribati
☐ July 12, 1979

Marshall Islands
☐ May 1, 1979

Micronesia
☐ November 30, 1978

Nauru
☐ January 31, 1968

New Zealand
☐ June 12, 1902

Palau
☐ January 1, 1981

Solomon Islands
☐ November 18, 1977

☐ June 24, 1971

Papua New Guinea

This flag was designed by a young art teacher just before the country became independent from Australia. The stars are the constellation of the Southern Cross, also seen on the Australian flag. The bird of paradise is the emblem of Papua New Guinea.

Tonga
☐ 1866

Tuvalu

The stars on the flag below represent the layout of the islands of Tuvalu. The coat of arms (on the left) contains the national motto "Tuvalu for God".

☐ October 1, 1995

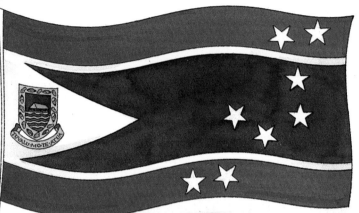

On the Tuvalu flag, blue stands for the sea, red for the achievements of the people and white for peace.

Western Samoa
☐ February 24, 1949

Vanuatu   ☐ February 18, 1980

On the flag of Vanuatu, above, the boar's tusk is a symbol of wealth. The crossed ferns mean peace. The "Y" shape stands for the layout of the islands.

Europe

Albania
☐ April 7, 1992

Andorra
☐ 1866

Armenia
☐ August 24, 1990

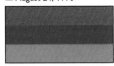

Austria
☐ November 12, 1918

Azerbaijan
☐ February 5, 1991

Belarus
☐ June 7, 1995

Belgium
☐ January 23, 1831

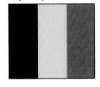

Bulgaria
☐ November 22, 1990

Croatia
☐ December 22, 1990

Bosnia-Herzegovina

Bosnia-Herzegovina broke away from Yugoslavia in 1990. It had never had a flag before, so historians had to look for <u>something</u> distinctive.

Cyprus
☐ August 16, 1960

The shield chosen is the emblem of the last King of Bosnia, from the year 1463.

☐ May 4, 1992

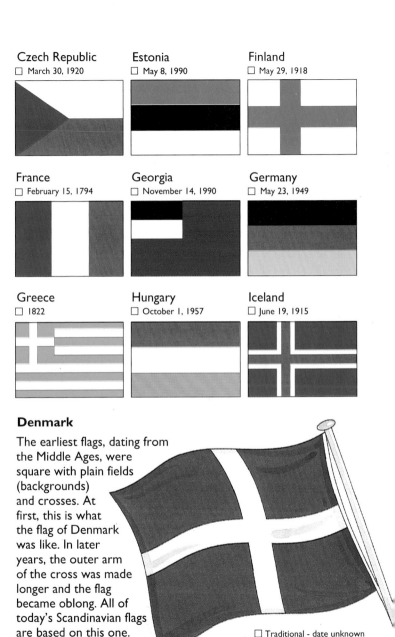

Czech Republic
☐ March 30, 1920

Estonia
☐ May 8, 1990

Finland
☐ May 29, 1918

France
☐ February 15, 1794

Georgia
☐ November 14, 1990

Germany
☐ May 23, 1949

Greece
☐ 1822

Hungary
☐ October 1, 1957

Iceland
☐ June 19, 1915

Denmark

The earliest flags, dating from the Middle Ages, were square with plain fields (backgrounds) and crosses. At first, this is what the flag of Denmark was like. In later years, the outer arm of the cross was made longer and the flag became oblong. All of today's Scandinavian flags are based on this one.

☐ Traditional - date unknown

17

Ireland
☐ January 21, 1919

Italy
☐ June 18, 1948

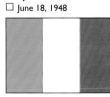

Latvia
☐ February 27, 1990

Liechtenstein
☐ June 24, 1937

Lithuania
☐ March 20, 1989

Luxembourg
☐ 1848

Macedonia
☐ October 5, 1991

Malta
☐ September 21, 1964

Moldova
☐ May 12, 1990

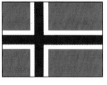

Monaco
☐ April 4, 1881

Netherlands
☐ February 19, 1937

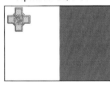

Norway
☐ July 17, 1821

Poland
☐ August 1, 1919

Portugal
☐ June 30, 1911

Romania
☐ December 27, 1989

Spain

When England and France were at war, Spain wanted a flag which was unlike either of theirs, so in 1785, red and yellow were chosen.

☐ July 19, 1927

Russia
☐ December 22, 1991

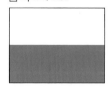

The Spanish flag often has the coat of arms in the yellow stripe, but this simpler form was invented in 1927.

San Marino
☐ April 6, 1862

Slovakia
☐ September 1, 1992

Slovenia
☐ June 24, 1991

Sweden
☐ June 22, 1906

Switzerland
☐ December 12, 1889

Ukraine
☐ September 4, 1991

United Kingdom
☐ January 1, 1801

Vatican City
☐ June 7, 1929

Yugoslavia
☐ April 27, 1992

North America

Antigua-Barbuda
☐ October 25, 1966

Bahamas
☐ July 10, 1973

Barbados
☐ November 30, 1966

Belize
☐ September 21, 1981

Canada
☐ February 15, 1965

Costa Rica
☐ October 21, 1964

Cuba
☐ May 20, 1902

Dominica
☐ 1988

Dominican Republic
☐ November 6, 1844

El Salvador
☐ May 27, 1912

Grenada
☐ February 7, 1974

Guatemala
☐ August 17, 1871

Haiti
☐ January 1, 1804

Honduras
☐ February 16, 1866

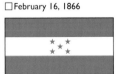

Jamaica
☐ August 6, 1962

Mexico ☐ September 16, 1968

In the middle of the Mexican flag lies a symbol from the Aztec civilization that existed in Mexico before the Spanish conquest in the early sixteenth century. It shows the pictogram (picture-word) for Mexico City.

Nicaragua
☐ September 4, 1908

Panama
☐ November 3, 1903

St. Kitts and Nevis
☐ September 19, 1983

St. Lucia
☐ February 21, 1967

St. Vincent
☐ October 21, 1985

Trinidad and Tobago
☐ August 31, 1962

United States of America
☐ July 4, 1960

South America

Argentina
☐ May 25, 1825

Bolivia
☐ November 30, 1851

Chile
☐ October 18, 1817

Brazil

The globe represents the night sky and the 27 stars represent the states of Brazil. The banner carries the national motto, which means "Order and Progress".

☐ May 11, 1992

Guyana

The flag of Guyana is known as the Golden Arrow, because the design represents an arrowhead pointing the country forward.

☐ May 26, 1966

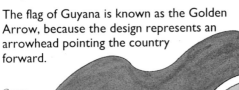

Green stands for Guyana's forests.

Yellow stands for its minerals.

Red stands for its people's energy and black for their staying power.

White stands for Guyana's rivers.

22

Colombia
☐ December 17, 1819

Ecuador
☐ December 5, 1900

Peru
☐ February 25, 1825

Surinam
☐ November 25, 1975

Uruguay
☐ July 11, 1830

Venezuela
☐ July 15, 1930

Paraguay

When this flag was designed in the 1840s, Paraguay had recently gained its independence after a revolt against its ruler, Spain. Red, white and blue were chosen because they were considered to be symbols of revolution.

☐ November 25, 1842

Regional flags

As well as standing for whole countries, flags can represent regions, provinces and states within countries. Many of these use local traditional emblems in their design.

The Union Jack

The Union Jack

The United Kingdom is made up of England, Scotland, Wales and Northern Ireland. Its flag, the Union Jack, is made up of flags which represent the patron saints of three of these countries – England, Scotland and Ireland. The flag of Wales is not represented on the Union Jack.

St. George's Cross of England

St. Andrew's Cross of Scotland

The flag of Wales – the Red Dragon

St. Patrick's Cross of Ireland

City flags

Some cities have their own flags, which are often based on heraldic symbols. These are traditional pictures and patterns, that were originally used to represent noble families in regions throughout Europe. The study of heraldic symbols is called heraldry.

The flag of Berlin, Germany's capital. The districts of the city replace the bear emblem with their own symbols.

State flags

Many countries are split up into smaller states or provinces which each have their own flag. The Australian state of Victoria, for instance, uses the emblem of the Southern Cross – a star constellation that can only be seen in the southern hemisphere. The Australian national flag also shows the Southern Cross.

The flag of Victoria, used since 1870.

The United Kingdom is split up into smaller areas, called counties. Many county flags may be many centuries old. The flag of Cornwall, for instance is also called the banner of St. Piran, who was the patron saint of tin-miners.

The flag of the English county, Cornwall.

The USA, Canada, Germany, Spain, Austria, Malaysia, the Netherlands, Brazil, Colombia, and Morocco also have regional flags.

The flag of the US state, California.

International flags

Some flags are not associated with particular countries, but with international ideas or organizations.

The Olympic flag

The Olympic flag is used at the Olympic Games, which are held once every four years. Athletes swear the Olympic oath while holding the flag and it remains flying throughout the event. At the end, it is lowered and sent to the city where the next games will be held. It was first used in 1920.

The Olympic flag. The rings represent the five continents.

The new Europe

The nations of Europe are working to promote closer links between them and the flag of Europe is seen more and more often. It stands for Europe as a whole continent. It represents perfection, not the first twelve member nations of the European Community as is often thought.

The United Nations

The United Nations is an assembly of world nations, formed to prevent war and organize peace settlements. It was set up in 1949 after the Second World War. Its flag shows a map of the world seen from above the North Pole, surrounded by olive branches, to represent peace.

The flag of Europe.

The flag of the United Nations.

Red Cross and Red Crescent

Medical staff, ambulances and hospitals often carry the sign of either the Red Cross or the Red Crescent. These represent organizations which give aid to victims of wars or disasters.

The Red Cross flag is used in countries where most of the people are Christian.

The Red Crescent flag is used in countries where most of the people are Muslim.

Flags for people

Some groups of people who share a common language, history and tradition do not have their own country. Sometimes, though, they do have their own flag. For instance the Sami, who live in Lapland (the northern parts of Norway, Sweden and Finland) have a flag.

The flag of the Sami. It is based on traditional art forms.

Corporate flags

Some international corporations have flags. This flag represents the motor racing team of Ferrari, the Italian car manufacturer, which exports cars all over the world.

The official Ferrari badge is shown in the middle of this flag.

Flags in history

Flags began as markers to identify armies and leaders, such as kings, queens and generals. Before cloth flags were invented, these markers took the form of fixed objects on poles.

The Romans

The Romans were the first to have a system of markers, known as standards, to identify their army. A standard was a fixed object, such as an eagle, on top of a pole decorated with badges. The standard was carried by a soldier called a standard-bearer.

The Romans also had a cloth standard called a *vexillum*, which flew from a staff like a flag, but which was fastened along its top edge, not the side.

The Roman vexillum

A Roman standard-bearer

The Crusades

Modern flags began around the time of the Crusades, when European knights journeyed to the Middle East to fight the Turks. King Richard the Lionheart (1189-99) of England used the symbol of three lions on his flag and wore it on his clothing and equipment. This symbol is still used today on the British royal standard – the official flag of the king or queen.

King Richard the Lionheart

Christopher Columbus

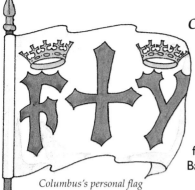

When Christopher Columbus discovered America, he carried two flags. One was the flag of Spain and the other was a personal one, given to him by the Queen of Spain. He flew both of these flags when he landed in the Bahamas on October 12, 1492.

Columbus's personal flag

Flags of America

When American colonists first rose against their British rulers in 1775, they used a British Red Ensign (a naval flag), with white stripes added across it to represent the thirteen colonies.

The first United States flag

After the Declaration of Independence in 1776, the Union Jack in the corner was replaced by a blue rectangle containing thirteen stars. This was the first Stars and Stripes.

The Stars and Stripes of 1776

When the American Civil War broke out in 1861, the Confederate states in the south split away from the northern states. Their first flag was called the Stars and Bars.

The Stars and Bars of 1861

French flag

Red, white and blue were adopted by French revolutionaries at the time of the French Revolution (1789-1792). They wore rosettes, called cockades. The modern French flag, called the *Tricolore*, is also red, white and blue. It was adapted from a French naval ensign of the 1790s.

The cockade worn by French revolutionaries

Make your own flag

Here are some ideas for how to design and make your own flags.

Design ideas

Before you begin to make your flag, think of some ways to decorate it. Draw the outline of your flag on a piece of paper and sketch out some ideas. Try using simple, bold patterns or symbols that would be visible from a distance. If you want to include writing on your flag, such as your name or your town, you could use a plastic stencil.

Paper flag

When you have decided on the design of your flag, you are ready to start making it. To make the paper flag below, you will need paper, pencils, felt-tip pens, adhesive tape and a large drinking straw.

1. Draw a rectangle approximately 10 x 20cm (4 x 8in) on a piece of paper. Cut it out. Make a fold 1.5cm (¾in) in from the left-hand edge.

2. Keeping the area to the left of your fold blank, draw the outline of your design with a pencil, so that you can erase any mistakes. Then, shade it in with felt-tip pens.

3. Turn the fold back and tape it along the edge to make a sleeve. Insert the straw – it should fit snugly. Add tape along the length of it and across the top to fix it in place.

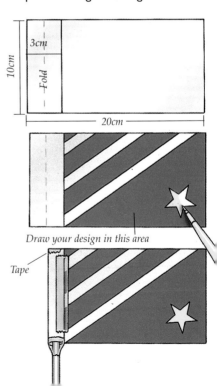

Draw your design in this area

Tape

Cloth flag

For this flag, you need: a piece of material, such as an old T-shirt or pillowcase; some fabric paints; household (PVA) glue; and a stick to attach the flag to.

1. Draw a rectangle as big as you can on one side of the T-shirt or pillowcase. Cut it out carefully.

Rectangle

2. Hem around the flag to stop it from fraying. With fabric paints, paint your design on one side of the cloth, leaving an undecorated strip (at least 3cm or 1.5in) along the left hand edge. Follow the maker's instructions on how to "fix" the paint to make it permanent.

Fabric paints

3. Cover the undecorated strip of material with glue. Place the stick as shown on the far left edge. Then roll it to the right. Stop rolling when you reach the edge of your design.

You could turn the flag over and decorate the reverse side, as if it were a mirror image, like a real flag.

Glue here

Roll the stick this way.

Index

First published in 1997 by Usborne Publishing Ltd, Usborne House, 83-85 Saffron Hill,
London, EC1N 8RT, England. Copyright © Usborne Publishing Ltd 1997
First published in America August 1997 UE